THE PATHFINDERS SOCIETY

THE PATHFINDERS SOCIETY

The **Mystery** of the **Moon** Tower

Francesco Sedita &
Prescott Seraydarian

illustrated by
Steve Hamaker

VIKING

VIKING

An imprint of Penguin Random House LLC, New York

First published in the United States of America by Viking,
an imprint of Penguin Random House LLC, 2020

Visit us online at penguinrandomhouse.com

LIBRARY OF CONGRESS CATALOGING-IN-PUBLICATION DATA IS AVAILABLE

ISBN 9780425291863 (hardcover)
ISBN 9780425291870 (paperback)

Manufactured in China

Book design by Steve Hamaker and Jim Hoover

1   3   5   7   9   10   8   6   4   2

Dedications

For Doug,

who makes so much seem possible,

and who keeps me on the path.   —FS

For C., B., and G.,

for giving purpose to my path. —PS

For my son, Alexander. —SH

1 Camp Pathfinder

2 Windrose Quarry

3 Merriweather Castle

4 Moon Tower

5 Moon Village

drose

MEET THE PATHFINDERS

KYLE is the new kid in town. He's always got a sketchbook in his pocket—and drawing is a very useful tool when you're connecting the dots on a treasure hunt!

BETH is super-organized and a bit of a history nerd. Need to go forward following a map? Or backward in time to solve a mystery? She's your girl.

HARRY is a goofball whose mouth sometimes moves faster than his brain. But his love of magic means he spots what's hidden in a tricky situation.

VICTORIA (VIC) is a popular cheerleader—and a secret math whiz. She figures out numbers and patterns along the path before anybody else even sees them.

NATE likes to invent stuff. His motto? A.B.R.: *Always Be Ready.* He's the guy you want on your team when you need solutions . . . *fast!*

13

14

16

21

26

28

31

32

33

35

PLUS ULTRA! A LATIN TERM THAT MEANS "MORE BEYOND!"

THAT'S WHERE WE HOPE YOU YOUNG CAMPERS WILL GO!

HENRY MERRIWEATHER'S PATHFINDERS SOCIETY AND THIS CAMP ARE BASED ON THE WISDOM AND KNOWLEDGE OF GREAT THINKERS AND EXPLORERS FROM AROUND THE WORLD.

41

MARLEY'S INN & GENE'S DINER

On this site stood the oldest known structure in Windrose, Originally Marley's Inn, a welcome haven for weary travelers. In 1816, a gentleman from Connecticut named Rensselaer W. Cowles came to Windrose to seek his fortune. In 1831, Mr. Cowles constructed the oldest portion of the inn as a private residence for himself and his wife. Mr. Cowles' life in Windrose was one of civil service and prosperity. As a resident he served as County Commissioner, Justice of the Peace and Postmaster, while also profiting as a merchant.

HUH, I NEVER REALLY NOTICED THESE TILE-MARKER THINGIES BEFORE.

WOW, YOU'RE A REALLY GOOD ARTIST, KYLE!

munch munch

THIS DOESN'T FEEL LIKE MUCH OF A TREASURE HUNT, BUT C'MON, LET'S FIND THE NEXT ONE.

FRY?

SO, NEXT IS THE CEMETERY?

I THINK SO.

48

50

51

53

54

55

56

LIKE HENRY MERRI--

I GUESS YOU COULD SAY THAT, YES.

ME TOO!

YES, OF COURSE, LIKE HENRY, UNCLE HENRY... WELL GREAT-UNCLE HENRY... AND HE *WAS* GREAT. YOU SAY YOU'RE FROM CAMP?

YOU'RE ALL PATHFINDERS THEN?

NO WAY!

I'VE BEEN AWAY FROM WINDROSE FOR QUITE SOME TIME. SO IT'S NICE TO SEE THE PATHFINDERS ARE STILL HERE.

AT LEAST FOR NOW.

HUH? WHAT'S THAT MEAN?

WHERE HAVE YOU BEEN?

BUMP

SORRY, OUR FRIEND DOESN'T USUALLY THINK BEFORE HE SPEAKS.

I MOVED AWAY YEARS AGO, BUT THEN I RECEIVED AN URGENT LETTER--A FINAL NOTICE.

NO MORE CAMP?

THERE IS NO MORE MONEY TO MAINTAIN THIS CASTLE OR THE CAMP. IT'S ALL BEING FORECLOSED. I'D NEED A FORTUNE TO STOP THE SALE--AND I DON'T HAVE ONE.

LET ME KNOW IF YOU KIDS FIND ANY TREASURE. *sigh...*

65

THIS WAS GREAT-UNCLE HENRY'S STUDY. WHENEVER HE FELT AT A LOSS OR NEEDED TO RECHARGE, HE WOULD COME IN HERE.

HE STRONGLY BELIEVED IN FINDING A PATH THROUGH THE MYSTERIES OF THE WORLD. HE KEPT SEARCHING RIGHT UP UNTIL HE LEFT.

WOW. MERRIWEATHER MADE ALL OF THE TILES?

THERE MUST BE LIKE A THOUSAND IN HERE.

ONE THOUSAND, FIVE HUNDRED, AND EIGHTY ONE.

UM, GIVE OR TAKE . . .

THERE'S THE MINOTAUR AND THE PILLARS OF HERCULES!

MY, YOU'VE GOT A GOOD EYE.

MY UNCLE LOVED MYTH AND STORIES. HE FELT THEY WERE MAPS TO THE HUMAN SOUL.

HE TRAVELED THE WORLD COLLECTING HIS FAVORITE TALES AND PUT THEM HERE, IN ONE PLACE OR ANOTHER.

81

86

tEERK...

IT LOOKS SAFE.

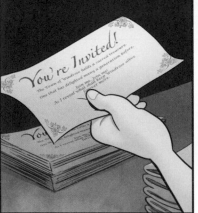

You're Invited!

The Town of Windrose holds a sacred treasure.
One that has delighted many a generation before.
Join me as I...and my
As I reveal what must be...
...

THERE MUST BE HUNDREDS OF THESE.

THAT'S NOTHING. LOOK AT THIS.

GASP!

"A WHO'S WHO WERE IN ATTENDANCE TO TOAST THEIR FRIEND AND HEAR ABOUT HIS DISCOVERY."

LADIES AND GENTLEMEN! THANK YOU FOR JOINING ME TONIGHT. . .

AS I UNVEIL TO YOU SOMETHING FROM WINDROSE'S PAST-- THAT WILL GUARANTEE ITS FUTURE IN THE HISTORY OF THE WORLD!

92

93

95

119

120

Chapter
SIX

128

PLUS ULTRA

Welcome to my workroom.
You're close to being through.
The next clue's a puzzle
that you have brought with you.

))))))●●●

The tiles may talk
If you arrange them just right.

THE TILES MAY TALK IF YOU ARRANGE THEM JUST RIGHT. USE THE RIGHT TOOL FOR ANOTHER TIME SIGHT.

WHOA!

TRY SOMETHING ELSE!

HOOOOOOOOMMMM

138

139

HOOOOOM!

143

147

STOP!

WHAT? THIS CAN'T BE. LOOK AT THE MAP, THERE'S NO LAKE HERE.

I THINK THIS LAKE WOULD DISAGREE.

WELL, I GUESS THAT'S IT THEN?

NO! IT CAN'T BE!

USE THE STONE TO CROSS THE SHORE . . .

151

152

155

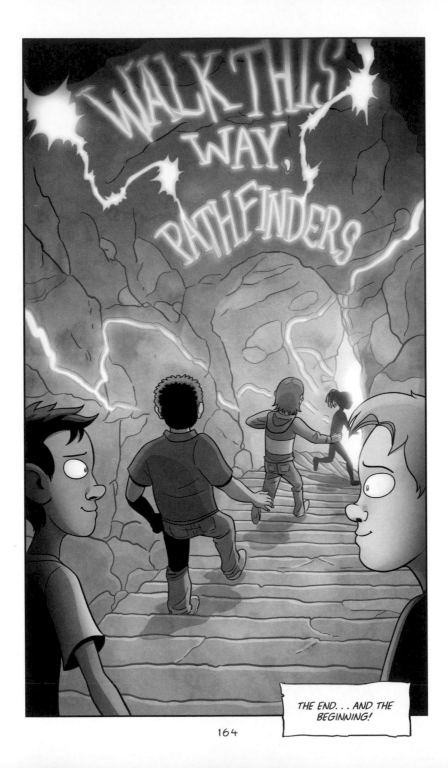

THE END. . . AND THE
BEGINNING!

To Be
Continued...

MEET THE AUTHOR

FRANCESCO SEDITA likes to make lots of things: this book is one of them. Other things he has created are the Miss Popularity books series, the Emmy Award–winning *Who Was? Show* on Netflix (which he made with his co-author Prescott Seraydarian), as well as lots of other books in his job at Penguin Young Readers, like Mad Libs, WhoHQ bestsellers, and other books with amazing authors like Henry Winkler, Lin Oliver, Giada De Laurentiis, and even Dolly Parton.

When he isn't making stuff, Francesco is cooking in his apartment in New York City or binge-watching a series with his husband or playing with their cute cat, Alfredo. Visit him at francescosedita.com.

Meet the Author

PRESCOTT SERAYDARIAN loves stories, always has. When he was a kid, he wrote stories about himself (and his entire neighborhood!) in endless enchanted adventures. That led to *telling* stories as a grown-up with amazing partners like Disney, Penguin, NBC, and Netflix through his award-wining film company Lunch Productions.

Now he has the best job of all as a film teacher at George School, a Quaker boarding school in Newton, Pennsylvania. Every day he gets to teach students (just a little older than the Pathfinders!) skills to share their own stories. Prescott lives at his school with his lovely wife, dynamic daughters, and endearing dog named Asher. Check him out at prescottseraydarian.com.

A Note from Francesco

THE PATHFINDERS SOCIETY is a series that I really never thought I'd write. There's more of an ending to this sentence—but first, I want to tell you a quick story.

Prescott and I went to college together. We quickly realized that we liked to write as a team and had a lot of fun entering TV contests. We never won, but we still kept submitting ideas. We even had internships at NBC at the same time. I worked at *Saturday Night Live* in the writing department, and Scott was just a few floors below in the NBC promotions department.

One day, after we finished college, I watched the Adam Sandler movie *Click*, where the main character has a remote control that can stop, start, rewind, and fast-forward his life. I immediately called Scott and said, "We should write *Click Part 2*!" And I was serious.

What he came back with was not what I expected. "We *should* write something together . . . but what if we write a TV show about five kids who are discovering who they are and what they're good at?"

And so we did. We had one rule: There had to be no pressure on this writing process at all. It took us a few years, but eventually we had a script for a TV show! We called it *The Young Professionals*. Our show took place in a small town, modeled on Prescott's hometown in Pennsylvania. The story was about five characters who meet and become friends during their internships, just like Prescott and I had.

We liked what we wrote and nervously asked a few people to read it. One of the readers recommended that we turn our script into a graphic novel.

A graphic novel?!

At first, we both said no. We'd spent a long time on the TV idea and I think we just needed some space. And then one night, while eating dinner together in New York City, we changed our minds.

Francesco Sedita (right) and Prescott Seraydarian (left) at the Mercer Museum in Doylestown, Pennsylvania

We decided that the story should be a bit different, too. Scott often talks about where he grew up and brought me to a museum near there called the Mercer Museum and Fonthill Castle. Something sparked: a new setting! Windrose and Henry Merriweather were born in our imaginations! It was all very magical, and I hope we've captured that feeling in these pages.

Okay, I'm going to try that first sentence one more time: *The Pathfinders Society is a series that I really never thought I'd write . . . without Prescott.* As we've worked on this first book, the town of Windrose has become a second home to us, and these characters that you've met are like our lifelong friends.

And I would never have written this without one of mine!

A Note from Prescott

IT'S FUNNY TO THINK ABOUT the paths that led here. Looking back, although every step was important, some felt a little more magical then others.

One of those first magical moments happened very early in the Francescott story, when we were both interning at NBC. Francesco had the exciting assignment upstairs but I had the cool view over Rockefeller Center. So at Christmastime, my office party was the place to be. I was allowed to bring one person, so I invited Francesco. When I think back now, we were barely older than the Pathfinders, but looking down on the dazzling sparkle of the enormous Christmas tree in Rockfeller Center, it felt like anything was possible.

That moment proved to be the start of working on many creative projects together. On that journey, the most magical moment happened when we asked ourselves "What if someone like Henry Mercer left a trail in the past for kids to follow in the future?"

If you don't know the name Henry Mercer, don't worry. But if you've read our story it may sound familiar. We based parts of the Henry Merriweather character on Henry Mercer, a real-world person and a bit of a local legend in the part of Pennsylvania where I grew up.

Henry Mercer was a man of many interests, from science and archaeology, to history, folklore, writing, and art. He was constantly curious about the world and its many connections. But he didn't just talk about it, he put his interests into action and his legacy lives on even today.

Mercer was born in Doylestown, Pennsylvania, in 1856. He grew into an exceptional student who could speak six languages. Henry was encouraged to travel, and he took a special interest in castles along the Rhine River in Germany. These castles touched something deep inside him, and so Henry dedicated himself to building one of his own.

The Mercer Museum and Fonthill Castle, and the Central Court inside the
Mercer Museum

The result of his hard work are two mysterious and beautiful concrete
castles, as well as a tile factory where Mercer pioneered the creation of
artistic tiles similar to those found in our book.

When Francesco and I discovered Henry Mercer, magic followed.
We were intrigued by so many things about his life, from his dog's
frozen paw prints in the cement castle, to his original keyboard, and
thousands of unusual tools that he collected in his own museum. But
it was Henry's love of exploration and interest in bringing history alive
that inspired our fictional character Henry Merriweather.

We hope our story is a lasting tribute to Henry Mercer and all
others who bravely set out to navigate the mystery, missteps, and per-
plexities of life in the spirit of "plus ultra!" Their courage has created a
little more inspiration for each of us to find our own way.

Meet the Artist

STEVE HAMAKER is the Eisner Award-winning colorist of bestselling graphic novel series such as Bone by Jeff Smith and Hilo by Judd Winick. He has also colored online comics series and created his own original web comic, PLOX. An avid tabletop and video gamer, Steve lives in Columbus, Ohio, with his wife and son. Follow him on Twitter @SteveHamaker.

A Note About Steve's Process

I get the authors' manuscript and sketch out the story so the look and the pacing are just right. The sketches go to the authors and editors. Sometimes we make changes.

2.

I redraw scenes if necessary and then trace over all the pencil lines in ink. I also do the final lettering.

3.

Now the magic happens: I add the color. Check out how lighter colors can make the stone and mushrooms "glow."

P.S. I do this all on my computer: 1, 2, 3 and we have a book!